PIRATE
PASSOVER

In memory of my grandmother, Clara Shaloum - J.P.

For Ian - A.G.

KAR-BEN PUBLISHING®
An imprint of Lerner Publishing Group, Inc.
241 First Avenue North
Minneapolis, MN 55401 USA

Website address: www.karben.com

Main body text set in Chaloops Reg.
Typeface provided by Chank.

Library of Congress Cataloging-in-Publication Data TK

Names: Press, Judy, 1944- author. | Gulliver, Amanda, illustrator.
Title: Pirate Passover / Judy Press ; illustrated by Amanda Gulliver.
Description: Minneapolis, MN : Kar-Ben Publishing, [2023] | Audience: Ages 3-8. | Audience: Grades 2-3. | Summary: As the pirates get ready for Passover, a storm washes their ship ashore, but luckily, they find a house with an open door, and everyone is invited in to enjoy the seder.
Identifiers: LCCN 2022015314 (print) | LCCN 2022015315 (ebook) | ISBN 9781728443034 (library binding) | ISBN 9781728443041 (paperback) | ISBN 9781728481241 (ebook)
Subjects: CYAC: Stories in rhyme. | Pirates—Fiction. | Passover—Fiction. | LCGFT: Stories in rhyme. | Picture books.
Classification: LCC PZ8.3.P9123 Pi 2023 (print) | LCC PZ8.3.P9123 (ebook) | DDC [E]—dc23

LC record available at https://lccn.loc.gov/2022015314
LC ebook record available at https://lccn.loc.gov/2022015315

Manufactured in the United States of America
1-50145-49814-4/25/2022

PIRATE
PASSOVER

Judy Press

illustrated by Amanda Gulliver

KAR-BEN
PUBLISHING

This is the story of a pirate named Drew
who sailed the high seas with a jolly good crew.

"All hands on deck!" Captain called to each one.

"Passover's coming! There's work to be done."

They swabbed the wood deck.

They shined the brass rails.

They cried out, "Heave-ho!"
as they raised the ship's sails.

"Get rid of the chametz!" Captain Drew loudly said.

"We'll have matzah for Pesach to nosh on instead."

With the sun almost setting and no time to wait,
Captain Drew was preparing the crew's seder plate.

A bowl of charoset, an egg that's hard-boiled,

karpas, maror, and a lamb bone that's broiled.

But the pirate crew noticed the waves roaring high,
as great bolts of lightning flashed through the sky.

Rain pounded the ship. It rocked side to side.

"A gale is upon us!" the frightened crew cried.

Matzah balls began rolling along the ship's plank.

Into the ocean they rolled. Then they sank.

The ship washed ashore. Out tumbled the crew.

"Follow me," said the captain. "I know what to do."

The door to one house was propped open wide.

A family was seated at a table inside.

"Shalom!" cried the captain. "You've nothing to fear.

Our ship ran aground and Passover's here!"

The pirates were welcomed—
invited right in!

"Tonight is our seder. Please sit.
Let's begin."

The candles were lit. The kiddush was said.

The karpas was dipped. The hagaddah was read.

Crisp matzahs were stacked. At first, there were three.

Then one disappeared. Now where could it be?

Captain Drew's parrot, Bernie, let out a squawk.

"I'll ask the Four Questions. I know how to talk."

They ate bitter herbs, as the story was told,

of the Jews leaving Egypt on their trek brave and bold.

The afikomen was found,
hidden under a seat.

Then they all sang "Dayenu"
and clapped to the beat.

They all waved goodbye as the pirates departed.

The weather was clearing. It was time to get started.

The storm clouds cleared up, with the moon shining bright.
And the ship sailed away on that Passover night.